THE SCREAMING OF
THE TYRANNOSAUR

STANT LITORE

MORE FROM STANT LITORE

THE ZOMBIE BIBLE

Death Has Come up into Our Windows
What Our Eyes Have Witnessed
Strangers in the Land
No Lasting Burial
I Will Hold My Death Close
By a Slender Thread (forthcoming)

ANSIBLE

Ansible: Season One
Ansible: Season Two
Ansible: Rasha's Letter

OTHER TITLES

The Running of the Tyrannosaurs

&

The Dark Need (The Dead Man #20)
with Lee Goldberg, William Rabkin

&

Lives of Unstoppable Hope
Write Characters Your Readers Won't Forget
Write Worlds Your Readers Won't Forget

THE SCREAMING OF THE TYRANNOSAUR

STANT LITORE

WESTMARCH PUBLISHING

2018

Text copyright © 2018 Daniel Fusch.

Stant Litore is a pen name for Daniel Fusch.

Cover art by Roberto Calas.

"The Screaming of the Tyrannosaur" was first published in 2017 in Samuel Peralts'a anthology, *Jurassic Chronicles*, a volume in the *Future Chronicles* anthology series.

ISBN: 978-1-7320869-0-6

You can reach Stant Litore at:
http://stantlitore.com
zombiebible@gmail.com
http://www.facebook.com/stant.litore
@thezombiebible

TABLE OF CONTENTS

for Inara

1

SEE ME. See what I can do. I walk naked out beneath the cameras with my sister athletes beside me, and the heat of these pounding sands would scorch my feet, but the nanites are already at work, toughening my soles, inuring them. For seven years they have shaped me, week to week and night to night—for speed, strength, sex appeal. For this moment.

My sisters sing a hymn to Hymen, god of marriage, but I only move my lips. I feel safe in my silence. It gives me time to prepare, to look up at all your faces. Your seats look like soap bubbles to me—bubbles high above my head, bubbles containing little circular platforms with people on them. Small hovercycles zip past with cameras, projecting our faces and bodies onto screens revolving slowly in the air near your bubbles, so that you can see us and those we are here to honor. The sands curve up to the left and right, along the curvature of this steel cylinder we're inside, and there is more sand yet high above your bubbles: we are spinning in space, though we don't feel the motion; the spin is what imprisons my feet to the sand. But gravity is not imprisonment, it is illusion. In a few moments, I will dance and leap in the air, competing with my sisters, and no chain will bind me—not gravity or any other. You will see what I can do.

This is a private dinodrome, chartered for races in honor of the wedding of the Duchess Amy Mardonia and the Third Lord Leo Archibald II. Tonight's is the last of the games; the celestial couple have already wedded and departed for the Bower; it is their guests who have remained behind that I and the animals will entertain. It is said that if one of the great creatures gives its death scream at the same moment as the consummation, the marriage is to be a lucky one. Of course, these matters are timed with precision, as all ceremonies are. A radio jock stands ready to transmit the games, play by play, to the Bower station, and the couple will time their sex so that the Duchess's virginity is not taken until the first death in the arena.

Everything in the universe yearns toward perfection of form and placement; this, my trainers have taught me. All things that are by their nature anarchic, wild, hectic, must be confined within tight steel walls and the tight strictures of ritual; only in this way can the human species be made beautiful and complete. Sex is by its nature an anarchic thing. So is laughter. So is aggression. The animals that will run with me in this arena in a few brief moments—they are the ultimate anarchic impulse, the ultimate sign of the containment of uncontrollable urges and the subjugation of the wild and organic to a specific aesthetic vision.

My own body is another such sign. As I wait here, perfectly poised, with my hook and its long coil of rope ready in my hand, I can feel my breasts shifting slightly as the nanites enlarge and lift them for your view. My skin feels oily and slick, not because I have applied any

Anyway, I have seen the others many times in training on the conservatory world, and in the small arenas of our training cylinder above Europa's frozen sea. I have no need to look at them; I know what they are like. Hyena is leaping and spinning in the air, unworried about wasting energy because her nanites will keep her going, and I can hear her throw her head back and yip each time she lands, like the animal whose sigil she's taken. Orca's dance is more alluring. Hummingbird is kneeling with her hands pressed together and her head bowed, swaying slightly; the delicate and non-functional wings grown to her back are whirring rapidly in the air, a blur of color behind her shoulders. She wants to suggest to you something of the virgin bride, as though her performance today will uniquely honor the young Duchess.

When the trumpets call, I simply bend to a crouch, one hand splayed in the hot sand before me, head lifted, ready for a sprint or a leap. I can hear the intake of your breath. Mine is the pose that draws you, because you have been talking for weeks about seeing the Timberwolf in action at last. The media has told you that I am faster than my sisters, that I am wilder, more savage, that I might be better. Now my stance promises you that you will see it.

On the screens above me, the Duchess Amy is enduring the fondling of her much older husband, but your gaze, and mine, is on the sands. I see the grit whirlpooling down some distance ahead of me, as the first of the trap doors is opened—I can't hear it, not over your screams—but I can see the dark opening in the bottom of this artificial world of sand and heat. Then the first triceratops comes up in a rush like a whale breaching, and

5

its loud call breaks the air. I leap forward into my run, and I *am* fast, faster than you knew, tearing across the sand toward the beast, my sister athletes hurrying behind me. Others surge up behind the first, but I ignore them. My hook flashes through the air; cold metal catches the frill just behind the beast's cheek. Even as it tosses its head I spring, using the bull's movement and my own momentum to carry me to its back, landing with my legs spread wide, one hand thrust into the air in triumph. I rock on its back. The beast roars, turning in a circle, but wrenching the hook loose from its frill, I spin the metal scythe on its rope in tight circles in the air. Then a quick lash, a cut across its flank sends my bull screeching forward across the sand. All your faces above me, all you in your bubbles, as I ride the rolling bull. One of my sisters leaps into the air to my left, and there are screeches behind me, and I know my competition is in pursuit. I will outrace them all.

We charge up the long slope of the dinodrome's hull, the first of many laps vanishing beneath us. The tug of spin gravity beneath us is fierce, but the tug of your applause is fiercer; the roar of it! I could leap into the air on it and fly, only I have to stay connected to my bull. Glancing back, I see Orca and Hummingbird and Hyena, each of them mounted, Hyena yipping and laughing, Hummingbird dancing, spinning in circles, flipping and catching herself on her toes on her bull's withers, her wings becoming streaks of light and color, like flame in the air. Orca intent. Intent on *me*, glaring forward; she is the closest behind me. The triceratops are in stampede, and there are more than four. Others race between us, and to distract your attention from Hyena's shrieks of joy and

Hummingbird's acrobatics, I spring from my bull's back to another's as it nears. I spin the hook and slash, driving it fiercely on, needing whatever bull I ride to be *first*. Orca follows, leaping high—leaping *over* my head—to her next bull. Then the others.

We charge past the ribbons of light and the blare of trumpets that mark the start of the second lap. I and the others leap and spin in the air from one bull's back to the next. The creatures surge and buck beneath us, maddened. Orca is the first to miss her leap, tumbling over the frill, but even as the triceratops tosses back its head and bellows its fury, she catches the animal's horn with her hands and spins around it to power a fresh leap to its back. Seeing the opportunity, I loop the hook rope about my own beast's horn and use it to tug my creature to the side, mid-charge, and it slams into Orca's bull just as she lands, half unsettled, on its back. She glances at me in horror as she topples back over the triceratops's hips and falls on her rump in the sand. Ignoring her, I loop the other end of the rope about her beast's horn, tethering the two together, and I flip in the air, dancing back and forth between the two bulls, wrenching raucous cheers from your throats. I am showing off, and you are loving it—this is what you came to see. This is how the mating bed of the Duchess and her groom is to be honored. And despite myself, I am laughing, laughing without control or pause: great giggles bursting from me as I leap and spin. I feel hot and full of oxygen and *alive*. Watch me leap onto the edge—*the very edge*—of a triceratops's frill and dance there, fast and nimble, my bare feet tapping lightly against the rounded rim of that huge shield the creature carries on its head.

Watch me cartwheel down its snout to balance precariously by one hand on the horn over its nostrils, before leaping back to the long horns above its eyes, where I spin and flip and twirl to amaze your hearts. Watch! Watch what I can do.

3

WE ARE RACING, pursuing each other in wide circles around the interior of the dinodrome, beating down the red sand. We crash through the insubstantial ribbons of the third lap, Hummingbird first, then I, then Hyena, and Orca last. You are all cheering, and I hear screams of *Hummingbird!* and screams of *Timberwolf! Timberwolf!* and even voices raised in howling and baying, attempting to drown out the humming that has started up now like a lightship's engines, the humming of those who've placed their bets on my competitor. I grin, lost in the noise of it all, the spotlights sweeping about, washing us all in violent colors. Somewhere on screens high above, the Duchess Amy quivers in Leo Archibald's arms, but I don't care. I am the center of your universe, not they, I and three other women, more skilled, more swift, more cunning and clever and agile than any others in the universe. It is to the rhythm of our pulse that you stamp your feet, to the rhythm of our breath that you chant. One camera shows you the Duchess and Third Lord whom we honor, but a thousand cameras show us. You have placed extravagant wagers on us; you know our bodies' measurements, you have speculated about the recipes for our perfumes—

perfumes engineered specifically for each of us; you know our sexual fantasies, or what we've been told to say those are. They're nonsensical, of course; every young man among you imagines being wanted by me, but Orca is more lovely and lethal than any of you are.

Anyway boys are forbidden us. Most everything is. Not one thing we've told your cameras comes from our hearts. All of it is engineered, shaped, perfumed for your consumption, as we are. Everything that doesn't please the cameras, that doesn't please you, has been waxed away. Even our memories. Above Europa they strip away everything they can during training, dressing us in identical leotards (when we're dressed at all), forbidding us the use of any language but Kartic, mandating attendance at the shrines of the sister goddesses Liberty and Love, forbidding us outside communication, and giving us sedatives early each evening so that we do not own even our dreams.

Yet I remember some things.

I remember bamboo bending in the wind. My mother's hands holding a cup of tea, lifting it so gently to my lips, the porcelain cool and clean. Letters drawn delicately on synthetic paper as my mother sings softly in my ear. A few stories whispered at bedtime, about a past before men and women could leap between planets. A small window that, when you looked through it, showed you an actual sky. Did I have a father? Siblings? That I can't remember. Not even the name of my family, only the name Mai Changying that everyone has called me during training.

When I was eleven, I asked Orca to share a memory of hers with me, and I would share one of mine. That was a mistake. My memory became a mockery in the mess, and the others took to chanting "China Girl, China Girl," whenever I walked in. We were to have one home, one only, in which to take fierce pride: and that home is our little station above Europa, where young women are trained as daughters of the goddesses. Other women look to the stars where we glint in orbit and yearn to be as beautiful, as strong, as desired as we are.

When I was twelve, I rebelled once.

I stood in the mess as they flung "China Girl, China Girl," at me, and with tears stinging my eyes, I sang a song from my childhood, as though to say in defiance: Look! My memories are beautiful. I like them. They are mine, they are not to be scorned!

When my trainer dragged me back to my cell, she made me kneel and slapped me, back and forth across the face, six times. My ears rang with it. I was crying. "When an eagle leaps into the sky," she demanded sharply, "does it yearn for the dirt it's left? Or does it swoop and hunt and stay up high above the weak, showing everyone the sky belongs to it forever?"

I didn't try again to make friends after that.

I learned to cry silently and without tears, in my room alone, as I waited for sleep. I held tight to my memories; they were a small secret inside me that no one could touch. And when the time came, I chose the timberwolf for my sigil, and tattooed not one on my body but three, together.

Now I imagine the other women and I are a pack in a running hunt through the snow, but the snow is sand, and my blood sings in my veins that I, and only I, must be first to our quarry. Hummingbird's bull is just ahead of me.

Lashing mine's flanks, I close the distance. I draw alongside her, and however she portrays herself for the cameras and for you, there is nothing innocent or demure in the glance she casts me, only hate hot as the nuclear furnaces that once baked a third of the earth. I grin at her. Then I am past her and she is yipping at her bull, lashing it on, but mine is faster, mine will *always* be faster. I am the best.

Orca passes her, too. Falling behind has enraged Hummingbird, and she is being too rough with the animal she rides. Orca is calm, focused, as I am. Then Hyena passes Hummingbird, too, and the two of them, Hyena and Orca, are both pounding after me, one to the left, one to the right. We crash into the fourth lap, and I keep my lead all the way to the fifth, but barely. All of you are screaming, my name or the others', all of you wild with the rush of the chase. As we careen across the sands on our final circuit of the cylinder, Orca and Hyena drive their bulls toward mine from either side, as though to crush me between them.

But I am ready. My hook spins through the air, and the rope coils swiftly about the right horn of Hyena's bull; a tug at the rope and a cry of dismay from Hyena, and the triceratops digs in its toes, trying to free its horn, but its momentum tumbles it into the sand. At a sharp cry from Hyena, I glance back quickly; a pang of relief as I see her rolling aside in a billow of sand, uncrushed.

Orca slams her bull's side into mine in that instant of distraction, but my bull keeps his footing. I deliver a hard tap of the metal hook against its snout. Grunting, the bull lowers its frill and drives its scaled cheek against its opponent's shoulder. Side by side, jostling each other, the two bulls charge through the darkness of disturbed sand filling the air. Orca grabs at my hair but I duck and try to sweep her with a kick. She leaps, too fast for that. I leap to her bull's back and—watch *this*—for a few moments we each try to dislodge the other, kicking, striking; then I catch Orca behind the heel and flip her off the bull, but she catches its horn in her hand and flips about it and she is in the air spinning. For an instant I catch my breath, admiring her grace. Then she lands on the other bull, the bull I'd ridden, and I laugh, for she is now without rope or hook. I duck and catch up the rope she's lost, the hook still caught on this bull's frill. One hand pushing against the frill, I retrieve the hook, then begin lashing the bull's flank.

In moments I have left Orca behind. Hummingbird is just behind me, but the cacophony of colored lights is ahead: the end of the race, just a few heartbeats ahead. My back and my thighs itch with sweat and a thousand particles of fine sand are stuck to me, but I barely notice. My head is back and I am baying my joy, as though I *am* a wolf. I hear the panting of Hummingbird's bull just behind to my left and I wheel on my bull's shoulder, bringing the hook scything on its long rope, hoping to dislodge her. Hummingbird ducks low and the hook sweeps through the air just over her head. Then she is in the air, leaping right at me. I spring back onto my hands and my right leg comes up and the kick is *so perfect*, my foot landing right between her breasts. She crumples, wheezing, and tumbles off the back of my bull into the sand.

There are explosions of color and light all about me, and howling; I rap the triceratops's cheek repeatedly with the cold hook. He veers to the left and we halt in a skidding plow of sand, just past the lap's end. Hovers zoom overhead with hundred-faceted cameras, and other bulls charge by, several without a rider, one with Orca, and the last with Hummingbird clinging to its thigh, where she must have leapt up from the sand, digging in her hook. But I laugh as they thunder past, because the race is done. It is *done*.

All of you erupt in shouts, slamming your feet, and handlers with shock rods rip across the sands on hovercycles, sparks flying as they goad the other triceratops toward gates at the arena's sides, gates already opening like hungry mouths. In the dizziness of colored floodlights and smoke from sudden firecrackers, I glimpse Orca and Hummingbird still astride their bulls, their faces red with rage or shame. Orca's eyes are wet. Then they are through the gates, and the gates are shut and the hovercycles are zipping away, and only I on my triceratops and all of you are left. Above me, a thousand small screens show my face, flushed and sweaty, and one large screen shows the Duchess with her back arched and the Third Lord crouched over her. Her face is flushed, too, and her eyes—for just a second I see her eyes—are bewildered.

Mine are not.

This is my victory. I have *won*.

I lift my hands high, my head back, letting your applause wash over me. For this one moment, I can close my eyes. I can just stand here on the bull's back, breathing.

A scream tears through your cheers, and I gasp. No one who has ever heard that scream ever forgets it. It is like no other cry. Like metal shearing. Like a station dying in orbit. Like a rip in time. A scream older and sharper than my cry of elation or your cry of worship. A scream that sent our ancestors trembling to their burrows when our forebears were still furred and quadrupedal and small enough to hold in your hand. The scream of a wounded and lonely thing promising violence and vengeance on whatever has hurt it.

Hearing it, I know the race, the run, was only a preliminary; your thirst for blood, all of you, has yet to be appeased.

I turn to face it.

There he stands, large enough to fill a temple's interior, his jaws parted in that toothed shriek.

Tyrannosaur.

4

THE TYRANNOSAUR'S SCENT is intense, an acrid musk like things dying on the edge of an ocean. This one is a bull, and the handlers have goaded him to aggression by spraying about him, likely for the past eighteen hours, the pheromones of tyrannosaur does in season.

Yet for all his heavy scent, the animal is beautiful. I find myself staring at him. He is stronger than his prehistoric predecessors, a little taller, his forearms even smaller, his powerful back legs bred for leaping. Fifty generations of revivified tyrannosaurs have preceded him, and selective breeding has made him a fierce giant of his kind.

But he is not beautiful because he is mighty. He is beautiful because he is sad. Look at him, standing there, his head moving in tight little jerks like a bird's, his feathers lathered in sweat. He keeps glancing about for the does he smelled. Maybe he hasn't slept in a day. They have toyed with him, his handlers, making him lust and sweat and breathe heavily, preparing him to run or to battle as they wish. When the game is ended, he will probably collapse from exhaustion, docile, drugged by his fatigue, and they will come at him with a sacrificial blade and loose his blood to spill across the sand. Immense as he is, this tyrannosaur, he is more a slave than I or my sisters.

His scream tells me that. See him tilt back his head, hear his screech like metal tearing apart. That is not a mating call; I have heard tyrannosaurs' mating calls. Nor is it a challenge, this roar that makes you all quiver with delicious fear, all of you who are protected in your high seats. No, that is a panic-cry, a terror-scream. The tyrannosaur is afraid. He is a wolf without a pack, and he is afraid.

A pang of regret, and I slash my hook across the triceratops's hip, urging it forward. With a recalcitrant bellow it lowers its head, frill like a wall, horns like spears, a mammoth of sinew and muscle and ivory charging toward the tyrannosaur. I will end this quickly. A few moments ago, I had wanted to prolong everything, to make this a night that every one of you, and not only the Duchess about to receive the Third Lord, will remember until your last breath. I may die in the games soon, or be cast aside when I am a year too old, but I would have you remember my name and my sigil.

Yet at this moment, my blood and my bones no longer beat with that fevered need. I long only to stop that tyrannosaur's scream, to end its pain, keep its aeons-old loneliness from sinking too deep into my heart.

5

I EXPECT THE CLASH to knock me from the triceratops' back, and I am ready to roll and rise and leap back before either beast can trample me, but no clash comes. The tyrannosaur springs to the left, and though the triceratops bends its head as if to catch a tendon with its horns as it passes, it makes no contact. The tyrannosaur darts in once we are past, osprey-quick, lunging for the soft, unprotected back of the beast I ride—and for me.

My adrenaline is too high for terror. I tug wildly at the rope, and the triceratops veers into a circle, following the pull on its horn. With a bellow it crashes into the tyrannosaur, its right hip against the carnivore's leg. I have leapt to its other hip, so I am not crushed between them. The tyrannosaur topples under the oncoming weight and he rolls aside in the dust; the triceratops stumbles to one knee.

"Up!" I scream at the bull. "Up!"

But the triceratops is shaking its head. Something has disoriented it. These animals have little vision, and in some the olfactory sense has been artificially impaired. And maybe there are other factors: some chemical soup the handlers injected into it, now reaching the end of its effectiveness and leaving the beast dizzy and sick.

"Up!"

The tyrannosaur gets his powerful legs beneath him and heaves himself back onto his feet, impervious to the bruises that must already be forming beneath the feathers on his leg. I hold my breath. His muscles bunch for a leap. I glimpse his eyes—those dark, dark eyes—and in them no longer any panic, only rage: the need to get to his females, the fury at whatever beast stands in his path. My sorrow for the creature wells up in me.

The triceratops wallows, wheezing, another moment in the sand.

And I make a choice.

As the tyrannosaur leaps, I leap too, springing from one beast to the other, hook in my hand. I sheathe the metal in the tyrannosaur's hide and dig my heels deeply into his feathers, and I am *riding* him.

Laughing.

No athlete has ever ridden one of *these*; we ride the herbivores that do battle with the toothed beasts. But I am riding this one, and truly, not one of you will forget this night.

The tyrannosaur dodges to the side, ignoring the triceratops, his head twisting to snap at me, at this pain on his back. I dance and leap on his shoulders, beveling on the rope, avoiding the snap and close of his jaws. My heart is suddenly full of rightness, a reckless liberty I haven't ever felt before. You and I are alike, I want to shout to the tyrannosaur. We should run together!

You all know the script for the games tonight: the triceratops gores the tyrannosaur, and a triumphant woman dances on the bull's back. But I have your script in my hands and I am ripping it in two. Because there will be a tyrannosaur and a woman together on the sand, everything else dead at our feet, and then I will ride this poor bull off the sands and back to wherever he sleeps, so that he may die, when they slay him, away from all your cameras and away from all your screaming faces. The handlers will want me punished for this, but you will all be shrieking my name and pounding your feet against the hull, and not even the gods will punish a woman whose name is in every mouth of every human being on this artificial world. This is how the games will go tonight.

I slash the tyrannosaur's right flank. Without a roar, with only a huff of breath, he turns, shakes his head, and charges again—right at the triceratops still half-kneeling in the sand.

"Come on!" I cry to the tyrannosaur bull I ride. "Come on! End it *your* way! Not theirs! Yours!"

6

THUNDER IN SPACE. We make it, the tyrannosaur and I, his great, taloned feet pounding down the long meters of this arena. I am whooping and laughing on his back, and though dozens of hovercraft flash with camera lights and floodlights of a dozen colors rush about me, no one can stop me. This is my moment. Mine and his.

My bull tears flesh, bleeding and red, from the triceratops's flank, long strings of sinew, baring white bone to the flare of light. Almost I can taste it between my own teeth. He rips his head back, almost flinging me off, but I dig the hook deep into his shoulder and bevel down his back. Then he and the triceratops are circling, and I am giddy. Near vomiting, near weeping. My body is being distorted from one second to the next as my nanites multiply desperately, striving to keep pace with my exertion. This must end soon.

In the vid I saw as a child, the wolves veered across the snow as smoothly as petrels over the water. All together, in silent, irrevocable grace. I wish other tyrannosaurs were here with us—that this beast I ride was not alone. He has only me, in this metallic universe that hangs like a jewel in the endless cold. Only me. An upward glance as we circle shows me the rotating screens: a dozen times reflected, myself and my tyrannosaur in a mist of red sand, blood streaming from his open jaw like ocean from the mouth of a whale breaching. On the screen there is no screaming crowd, no space cylinder, just sand and flesh: two wild animals naked—woman and immense, feathered bird. The triceratops offscreen preparing for its next charge. As though we are in a wilderness and are not captives owned and shaped for your cameras. At those screens, I burn hot with anger. Those wolves in the vid—they were the same, bounded within some narrow sanctuary or zoo, though the screen revealed to my childhood eyes neither cameras nor fences. I know this now. They were as severed from European forests as I am severed from China, and their union in a pack was a thing both temporary and fragile. Even on the beaten worlds beneath us, farther down the sun's gravity well, nothing real remains. Everything is shaped for the cameras. Even you yourselves.

But the tyrannosaur, my tyrannosaur, is no longer screaming.

There is blood on his jaws.

He is angry now, not afraid.

Only you up there—only you are still screaming.

He pants as we circle, stirring the sand. Sweat runs over my skin. I breathe through my mouth. The triceratops drags one hind foot and snorts sand from its nostrils in explosions of breath. "Now," I whisper, and lash my tyrannosaur's flank, sending him into a run. His hunting cry is long and ululating and my whole body, marrow and bone, reverberate to it. For the briefest instant I wonder if Orca, Hyena, Hummingbird are watching me on the screens, if they can see my hair in the wind, if they can hear me whooping with the tyrannosaur bull. We close with our opponent in a crash of feather and hide.

The triceratops feints—I see it, my bull doesn't—then slams its head into my tyrannosaur's hip. I flick my hook across his cheek to warn him, too late. Two spires of ivory shear deep. My ears would bleed at the bull's scream, so near my own head, but the nanites stanch the blood before I ever feel it. Eardrums are easily repaired, more so than lungs or entrails or hamstrings, and the living galaxy of tiny physician machines burns hot and fast inside me. Not so with my tyrannosaur; no devices smaller than mitochondria inhabit or protect him. He is designed to die.

A tower of muscle and sinew, he founders.

I dance across his shoulders, but he is falling, and all I can do is spring aside to land in a blossom of sand and red dust. His crash sends a hot cloud of it at me. Still he screams as he kicks his fierce leg, throwing up more sand. The triceratops charges by me, a wind against my body. Balancing on my feet, I join my scream to the tyrannosaur's as the frilled beast slams again into his belly. There is a deeper red than the sand.

My body is hot and my breath is hot and I am cooling in a sheen of sweat, but for the fury in me there is no cooling. My tyrannosaur flails weakly in the sand. I have only a second to think and I do not use it. There is no thought, only rage. Gripping the handle of my hook, I hurl myself into the air, leaping to the triceratops, onto its shield of bone.

7

THIS DAY HAS GONE long enough without a death. Clinging with my thighs to the edge of the triceratops's frill, I spin my rope beneath and around its neck, then leap across to the bull's other shoulder to catch the hook, and as I tighten the noose, the beast gives a hoarse roar and breaks into a panicked run, clouds of red sand billowing past me like architites blowing on the wind over Neptune's second sea.

I dance grimly on its back to keep my balance, and the muscles scream in my arms. I do not care if I damage myself; the nanites will repair me. My pulse is beating hot in my temples and all I can think of is to tighten, tighten that rope.

With a gasp, the triceratops stumbles to its knees; it shakes its head as if to throw me, but I stay put. Its horns sweep past before my eyes like trees in a gust. I sit and slam my feet against its frill for leverage and I pull and *pull* at the rope. Red and purple light washes across me, garish, from the hovers, but no one interferes. All of you are watching, I can feel your lust wash up in waves against me, your yearning to see one of us naked animals down here, at least one of us, die a gory death.

I give you no gore with this one; you have had enough blood. The triceratops's tongue hangs from its mouth and its huge sides lift and fall raggedly and then are still as I cut off the last of its air. It gets uneasily to its feet, a surge of its muscled body beneath me like the whole earth moving, but then the beast beneath me tilts and it collapses onto its side, a bow wave of sand cresting away from its fall. I leap free, hitting the sand and then somersaulting back through the air to land again on its thigh, and I am pulling the ropes taut again, so taut, allowing it not one gasp. It kicks weakly, craning its head back, the great frill scooping sand before it like some monstrous shovel. I neither speak nor shout; I just strain at the rope, letting the nanites within me heighten my muscles and hyperoxygenate my veins, giving me such strength and endurance as you have only in your dreams.

The triceratops stops kicking, the death noise in its throat loud like rocks rasping together. I do not relax my hold. Then it shudders and is still, and as all of you hold your awed silence, from a thousand megaspeakers the Duchess Amy Mardonia's sharp cry pierces the air: the act of love a ceremonial refutation of the day's first death.

Numb, I slide from the triceratops's hip, barely noticing the impact of the sand against my feet. I leave my rope and hook wound about its neck. The triceratops lies lifeless behind me, of no more significance than an unnamed boulder in the hills. My fury still burns through me like forest fire through bamboo, but I no longer care about that horned beast. I give no heed to the Duchess Amy's moans or to the excited cheering of your tens of thousands that soon drowns her out. There is only one I care about now, and my eyes are on him as I cross the sand.

8

THE TYRANNOSAUR, my tyrannosaur, lies gored and dying; I walk to his head. As I bend to look into his eye, already glazed with pain and approaching entropy, the roar and rush of all your voices fades until it is nothing louder than the rush of my own blood in my ears.

It is over. I am not yours anymore to prize, or envy, or yearn for, or fuck. None of you matter.

Tenderly, I kneel by his massive head and put my arms around him. His head is warm against my breasts, his feathers soft. He makes a wheezing sound but does not move at my touch.

He has been trained and shaped, too. He has been torn from his place and time as surely as I have. And I wonder that none of you, not one of you, has thought to pity him. I can see into his heart. I make him a vow, whispering the words in Mandarin near the tufted hole of his ear. I will teach my sisters to see into his heart. Into all your hearts. As I have.

Embracing the dying bull, I sing softly to him a song of my mother's, a song of old China, words of Li Po's set to music long before I was born, in a year when there were only moons in the sky and no orbital platforms, no conservatory worlds or steel cylinders. Maybe only one moon; I think there was only one moon made by the gods and not by men.

My voice is softer than I have heard it before; tears burn at my eyes.

Among the blossoms I
am alone with my wine;
lifting my cup I ask the moon
to drink with me, its reflection
and mine in the wine, just we three:
and I sigh, because the moon cannot drink
and my reflection just mimics me, silent;
no other friends here, these two
alone are with me—

The tyrannosaur murmurs low in his throat, like a child about to shift in his sleep, and I know this beautiful old animal understands the song. At least as much as I do. More than any of you ever will. Yearning takes me, to retrieve my metal riding hook and plunge it into my own breast, to bleed out here beside the tyrannosaur and leave all of you behind, all of you lost in the scream of your crowd. Because I am a wolf separated from her pack, watching my only companion die.

But I have made a promise.

As the hovers approach with a roar like cicadas at dusk, I cling tightly to my tyrannosaur's head, close my eyes, and sing softly as I weep.

FINIS

THE SCREAMING OF THE TYRANNOSAUR

IF YOU'VE ENJOYED
THIS STORY...

Competition is fierce on the backs of charging tyrannosaurs. And today, young Egret will compete with other tyrannosaur riders aboard a far-future colosseum. In space. Read her story for FREE.

CLAIM A FREE COPY of *The Running of the Tyrannosaurs*:

BookHip.com/CBFQAP

Downloading your copy of this next novelette, you'll also join my readers' group, so that you'll receive updates when the next book comes out! *The Running of the Tyrannosaurs* is also available at Amazon and (in paperback) at Barnes & Noble Online.

Next up in the series: *Nyota's Tyrannosaur*, a novel set on the Conservatory World where the tyrannosaurs and other species are grown and where Liberty's daughters are prepared for life in the arena.

ACKNOWLEDGMENTS

I REALLY LOVED writing this story—both because of a lifelong obsession with dinosaurs that I never entirely grew out of (who am I kidding, I didn't grow out of it *at all*), and because it was an opportunity to work out my fury at our beauty culture and our entertainment culture. As a father of two daughters, the way our culture distorts the lives of young women is often pressing on my heart. Then, too, I wanted to tell a story of unexpected kinship, of finding a companion in an unexpected place when alone. And if that companion is feathered and weighs nine tons, well, that's par for the course when you're writing science fiction. I owe a debt of gratitude to all those who helped this story happen—to Jessy Pace for her meticulous help with research, to Crystal Pikko Watanabe for her generous and thoughtful developmental editing, to Samuel Peralta for including the story in its first appearance in his anthology *Jurassic Chronicles*, to Roberto Calas for the gorgeous cover art, to Jessica my wife for vigorous encouragement—I could not have done it without you. And also, my deep thanks to all the fans and beta readers who clamored for another story set in the world of *The Running of the Tyrannosaurs*. There is more to come; I am now working on a novel, *Nyota's Tyrannosaur*, which I think you will enjoy very much. Thank you for believing in this series.

ABOUT THE AUTHOR

STANT LITORE WRITES about zombies, aliens, and tyrannosaurs. He does not currently own a starship or a time machine but would rather like to. He lives in Aurora, Colorado with his wife and three children and hides from visitors in the basement library beneath a heap of toy dinosaurs, tattered novels, comic books, incomprehensibly scribbled drafts, and antique tomes. He is working on his next novel, or several. You can read some of his current fiction by looking up *Ansible*, *The Running of the Tyrannosaurs*, *The Zombie Bible*, or *Dante's Heart*. However, doing so may have unpredictable effects, and Stant offers no assurances that you will emerge from any of these stories unscathed. Best leave all non-essentials behind, take with you only what you need to survive, and venture into the books cautiously and ready to call for backup. Enjoy, and good luck.